Run, Jimmy, Run

Malachy Doyle

First published 2011 by
A & C Black, an imprint of Bloomsbury Publishing Plc
50 Bedford Square London WC1B 3DP

www.acblack.com
www.malachydoyle.com

ISBN 978-14081-4259-2

A CIP catalogue for this book is available from the British Library.

This book is produced using paper that is made from wood
grown in managed, sustainable forests. It is natural, renewable
and recyclable. The logging and manufacturing processes conform
to the environmental regulations of the country of origin.

Printed and bound in Great Britain
by CPI Cox and Wyman, Reading, RG1 8EX

recommended by

www.catchup.org

Catch Up is a not-for-profit charity which
aims to address the problem of
underachievement that has its roots in
literacy and numeracy difficulties.

RUN,
JIMMY,
RUN

Contents

Chapter 1

Do As You're Told!

"Run!"

I turn and run.

"Stop! Don't move!"

I stop dead. My feet stick to the floor, but I feel as if I'm falling.

I don't fall. Somehow I stop myself, just in time.

Then a knife flies past, just in front of me. Just where I'd have been if I'd still been running.

"Run!"

I run again.

"Stop!"

I stop.

"Run! Stop! Run! Stop!"

I stop dead every time. I stop because knives are flying at me from the left and the right, from above me and below me.

So I do as I'm told. Exactly as I'm told.

I come to a door.

"You're learning, Jimmy. Now go inside!"

I go in. It's dark. I can just about see a light switch. I reach up…

"Aaahh!"

The light gives me an electric shock. I fall to the floor.

"No one told you to switch it on!" The voice is all around me. "Do as you're told and nothing else! Now climb up the stairs!"

I climb all the way up, to the very top of the building.

"Now open the door. The one above you!"

I look up. It's a heavy metal door. I'm only just strong enough to push it open.

"Go through the door and walk forward!"

I climb out onto the roof and start walking. I walk all the way to the edge.

"Open your arms wide!" the voice demands.

I open my arms wide.

"Now fly!"

I lean forward.

And fall.

And fall.

Chapter 2

Never Coming Back

I wake up.

"Out of bed now, Jimmy!" shouts my mum. "It's time for school!"

No way am I going to school. Not today. Not ever again.

I jump out of bed and throw on my clothes. I grab my rucksack and go downstairs. I eat my breakfast, kiss Mum, and then I go out.

I am never going to come back.

No more getting on the school bus.

No more facing Dax and the gang at the school gate, taking my dinner money.

No more going hungry at lunchtime.

No more feeling faint in the afternoon, because I haven't had any lunch.

No more getting shouted at by the teachers because I am falling asleep.

No more looking out for Dax and the gang all day. No more wondering what they will do to me next time.

No more of any of it because, early in the morning, before they woke up, I'd crept into Mum and Dad's bedroom and taken £150 from Dad's wallet.

Then I packed a rucksack full of clothes and food and stuff.

Now it's 8.30 and I'm gone. Safe. Free.
Away.

I get on the number 49 bus and go to the train station. At the ticket office there, I buy a ticket. "Newtown," I say.

"Single or return?" asks the man.

"Half single, please," I say.

I get on to the train and keep my head down till the train pulls out. I've done it. I'm free.

The train rushes past the glass factory, past the chicken farm, past the hospital. Past everything that was home for the past 13 years.

I need to change out of my uniform so I get up and go to the toilet. I take my rucksack and change my clothes in there.

And on the way back, there he is! It's Dax!

I dive into a seat. Did he see me? No. I don't think so.

I sneak another quick look to be sure it's him. And it is. He is reading a magazine. He has headphones on. There's a cruel smile on his face.

Someone has left a newspaper on the seat. I pick it up and hide behind it.

I can't stay here. He is sure to see me.

I wait till the next station. Then I get to my feet. I use the newspaper to hide my face. I grab my rucksack and jump down off the train.

Run, Jimmy, run!

I dash to the far end of the train and climb back on just as the doors are shutting. I make my way to the last seat and sit facing the wall. There is no one else in the carriage.

I hide my head in the newspaper.

Chapter 3

Tickets, Please!

"Well, if it isn't Jimmy Chicken Smith!" says Dax.

He grabs the newspaper from my hands and smacks me round the face with it.

"You can't hide from me!" he says. "Are you bunking off school? A good little boy like you! Wait till I tell the Head about this!"

"What about you?" I hear myself saying.

"Me? I'm going to the dentist."

Dax grins at me. He's got metal braces on his teeth.

"Mind you, maybe I won't bother to go to the dentist. Maybe I'll come along with you instead. Where are you off to? Are you meeting a girl? I bet you're running away! Come on, you can tell your old friend Dax. Your secret's safe with me."

And he grins at me again.

Why didn't I run for it while I had the chance? Why did I get back on the train?

At least Dax doesn't know about the money. I glance up at my rucksack, to check it's safe.

Dax sees me do it.

"What's in there, then, Jimmy boy?" he says.

"Don't you dare!" I say, and I push him away. Dax hits me back.

And at that moment the guard comes into the carriage.

"Stop that, you two," he says. "Tickets!"

I put my hand into my pocket.

"That's mine!" yells Dax to the guard. "He just nicked it off me! He saw you coming and grabbed it. He hasn't got one, see."

The guard takes my ticket, stamps it, and hands it to Dax.

"Ticket?" he says, looking at me.

"But…" I say.

"No ticket, no travel," says the guard. "Do you want to pay, or do you want me to call the transport police to meet us at the next stop?"

I put my hand in my rucksack and find the wad of notes. I hand over a tenner and the guard gives me a ticket.

I put the rest of the money deep into my trouser pocket.

Dax is watching every move I make.

* * *

"This is my lucky day!" says Dax.

The guard has gone. The train is pulling into the next station.

I wait till the doors are about to shut, then I grab my rucksack and run.

Run, Jimmy! Run!

Dax sticks out his foot. I go flying, crash into someone, and land flat on my face.

"Hey! That's not very nice!" says the man I bumped into.

"Sorry! Sorry!" I say.

"Not you," says the man, helping me to my feet, as the train starts to move again. "Him!"

He turns to Dax.

"I saw what happened," he says to Dax. "This boy was trying to get off and you tripped him up. You sent him flying into me, and now he's stuck on the train. So, do you want to explain yourself, or shall I go and fetch the guard?"

"He's my brother," Dax tells the man. "He's a bit simple. Not quite all there, if you know what I mean."

The man looks at him. Then he looks at me.

"I'm looking after him," says Dax. "Our father's meeting us at the next stop. But Jimmy thought it was this station. I had to stop him."

I know the man is going to believe Dax, so I put my rucksack on the luggage rack.
I sit down, next to Dax, and wait till the next station.

When the train pulls in, the man stays on. Dax and me get off, like we're together. Like he's looking after me.

And as soon as I set foot on the platform, I run like hell!

Chapter 4

Bus Chase

Run, Jimmy, run!

I can hear Dax right behind me. I will never outrun him.

Then I remember I've left my rucksack on the train. Now I have no clothes and no food! It's lucky I put the money in my pocket.

I flash my ticket at the inspector. Carry on running.

"Hey, you! Stop!" shouts a voice.

I look round. They're shouting at Dax, not me. The inspector has grabbed him.

I race on, out of the station. A bus is pulling out so I jump on.

"Town centre," I say, tossing some coins at the driver.

Dax is coming out of the station. He sees me on the bus. He looks very, very angry.

He turns to look behind him. I look, too.
Another bus is just about to pull in.

It's going to the town centre too. Would
you believe it?

Dax's bus is right behind us. It stops at the same places as my bus. I can tell Dax wants to get off. He wants to run and get on my bus before it pulls out again. Only he's scared he'll miss it and I'll be gone.

I wait till my bus pulls in to a stop where there isn't enough room for both of them.

Dax's bus will have to wait in the road till my one pulls out again.

I jump off as soon as the door opens.

Dax bangs on the door of his bus.

But the driver won't open it until he's pulled in to the bus stop.

Dax is shouting at his driver. I can see he's really angry.

I'm out on the pavement. Now Dax is shouting at me.

"I'll get you, Smith!" he's saying. He has his fist up against the glass. "Just you wait!"

And I run. I run into the shopping centre. I run as if my life depends on it.

Maybe it does.

Chapter 5

Clothes Shopping

I run into a clothes shop and grab the first thing I see. A pair of bright pink jeans! I go into the changing room and pull the curtain shut. Dax won't be able to see me now.

I decide to try the jeans on in case the
assistant wonders what I'm up to. They're
about ten sizes too big.

The next moment, I see a face above me.
It's Dax! He's in the next cubicle, standing on
a chair!

"Hey, you!" The shop assistant must have seen Dax. "What do you think you're doing?"

And I run.

Run, Jimmy, run!

The pink jeans are down around my knees by the time I'm out the door of the shop. I've no shoes on. The alarm's beeping, and that means a security guard will grab me any second now.

And my money's still in the cubicle, in the pocket of my trousers!

I have no choice. I go back in.

"It's OK," I say to the shop assistant. "It's only a game. He's my brother."

She looks at Dax. Then she looks at me.

"Are you buying those jeans?" she asks me.

I shake my head, and kick the jeans off, right there in front of her.

"I didn't think so," she says.

I'm standing there in my pants. She doesn't know if she should shout or smile.

"Can I put my trousers back on?" I ask her, pointing to the changing rooms.

"Yes," she says. "I think you should do that."

I come back out and give her the bright pink jeans.

"Sorry about that," I say.

Dax is still there, waiting for me.

"Not buying them, little brother?" he says, grinning. "Shame. They suit you!"

We go out of the shop together.

Chapter 6

Thud!

"Right, kid." Dax has got me by the arm. "Hand over your money. All of it. Now."

I reach into my pocket. Then I spot a gap in the traffic.

And I run!

I get to the middle of the road. There's a lorry coming towards me on the other side.

Should I wait or run? I risk it.

I get to the other side. Then I hear a screech of brakes. I spin round. There's Dax. He's moving towards me as if he hasn't a care in the world.

Run, Jimmy! Run!

I race down the pavement and into a shopping mall. I go up the escalator and dash into a bookshop.

Dax is still right behind me.

He tries to grab me, and books go flying onto the floor. People are staring at us.

Dax grabs hold of a bookshelf to do a quick turn, as I run back up the other side. More books fall off.

I duck past the manager, who's trying to block the doorway.

"Stop!" he's yelling. "*Stop!*"

I see a lift. The door's shutting.

I dash in just before the door closes and drop to my knees, gasping for breath.

The door opens. We're on the ground floor. Dax isn't there.

I run back out onto the street. I spot a gap in the traffic and run across the road. I get to the other side, but then I hear a screech of brakes and a thud.

The street goes silent. I spin round.

A bus has stopped dead in the middle of the road. On the ground, in front of the bus, there's a pile of clothes.

It's Dax.

Nobody moves. Then the driver climbs down from his cab. He's bending over Dax and pulling out his mobile.

"Ambulance. High Street. Fast!" he says.

What do I do now?

Run, Jimmy?

Run?

Chapter 7

Under the Bridge

I walk out into the middle of the road. All the traffic has stopped. A crowd of people are around Dax.

"He came out of nowhere!" The bus driver looks shocked.

"I felt this bump and I saw a bundle of clothes," the driver goes on. "He must have just hit the side. He can't be… Surely he can't be…"

"Dead?" Dax opens one eye. "No way!"

He sits up and looks around. He sees me and grins.

"Help me up, little brother!" he calls.

"Don't move!" the driver tells him. "There's an ambulance on the way. You're not supposed to move."

"I'm fine," says Dax, and he gets to his feet. He's leaning on me. "Let's go, Jimmy!" he whispers. "Run!"

And we run. Sort of.

We can hear the sirens, coming closer. People are shouting. Some of them come running after us. But we run. And no one stops us.

We run and hop and hobble, till we're well away.

We go down to the canal and stop under a bridge. Dax slumps down and sits on the path.

"You all right, Dax?" I say. "Are you really all right?"

He looks up and grins at me.

"Course I am, brother," he says, with a wink. "The bus never hit me at all!"

I stare at him. "But I heard it hit you," I say.

"I ran into the bus on purpose," says Dax. "It was only going slow – you know what they're like. I thumped my fist against the driver's door, as hard as I could. Then I threw myself to the ground, well clear of the wheels."

"But… why?" I ask.

He looks at me, grinning. "It stopped you in your tracks, Jimmy boy, didn't it?" he says. "Now I've got you where I want you. You're here, with me, alone. You and that big wad of notes you've got stuffed down your trousers."

Time to run again, I'm thinking.

But he's giving me a funny look. "Only…"

"Only what?" I say.

"Only now I've got you, I can't…" He looks away. Stares into the canal.

"What can't you do?" I ask him.

"I can't seem to… Not when you…" Dax mutters.

"Not when I what?"

"You came back for me, Jimmy boy," says Dax. "You could have run, and you didn't. You came back to see if I was all right."

"But that's what you wanted me to do," I say.

"Yeah, but…" Dax frowns. "I didn't really think you would. Why did you?"

"I had to." I shrug my shoulders. "I thought you were hurt."

"Yeah."

There's a long silence.

"But would I have come back for you, if you'd been hurt?" Dax looks up at me.

"Would you?" I ask him.

"I don't know." He shakes his head. "That's it, you see. I don't know."

Chapter 8

Running

"Let's see the money, then," says Dax.

I reach down into my pocket and pull out the wad of notes.

"How much have you got?" he asks me.

"£150, minus the bus and train fares,"
I say.

Dax whistles. "Where did you get it?"

"My dad."

"You nicked it?" He looks sort of
shocked.

I nod and stuff the money away again.

"You nicked it because of me?" he asks.

"To get away from me and the gang?"

I nod again, slowly.

We both stare at the canal.

"So where were you off to? What were you going to do?" asks Dax.

I shake my head. I don't know.

"Were you really running away?"

"I dunno," I say.

"So what about now?" he says. "What are you going to do now?"

I shake my head again.

We're both staring at the water.

"I think we'd better go back," he says.

"Back where?" I ask.

"Home. School. All that," says Dax.

"And give the money back?" I ask.

"Yeah." He nods.

"And carry on as before?"

"How do you mean?" he asks.

"You and me," I say.

"Yeah, sure," he says. "Well, no. Maybe. We'll see."

"We'll see?" I ask.

"We'll see, little brother." He looks up and grins. Only the grin looks just a bit different, this time. More like a proper smile.

"So are you going to the dentist?" I ask him.

"Not today," he says, shaking his head. "I just fancied a day off school, like you."

I think about what he's said. *Yeah. No. Maybe. We'll see.*

"OK." I get to my feet now. "Let's go."

Then, "Let's run!" I say, as we come out into the light.

So we start running together.

Me and Dax.

We're running.

Beast Hunter

When Jacob spots a crocodile in the old quarry, nobody will believe him. He needs to get a photo as proof before anyone will listen to him. And that means hunting the beast himself!

ISBN 978-1-4081-4265-3
RRP £5.99

Death Match

While the Nazis occupied Ukraine,
Dynamo Kiev's footballers played matches as
FC Start. Start won, again, and again. Until
they faced a German army side, under the
threat of death if they didn't let the occupiers
win...

ISBN 978-1-4081-4263-9
RRP £5.99

The Haunted Mobile

Jake's mobile is going wrong. It's sending weird texts to his friends. Then they start to appear on his phone – from himself. A strange girl keeps calling him. He knows he has to track her down. But by the time he finds her, will it be too late for the girl – or for Jake?

ISBN 978-1-4081-4258-5
RRP £5.99